Moments with Massy ™ series is dedicated to my amazing grandchildren Massilon , Max, and Adrienne. They were my advisors and creative team every step of the way for Moving Away Will Be Okay!

Kellie Carte-Sears

Moving Away Will Be Okay!

D1439570

Written by   Kellie Carte-Sears

Moments
with
massy
™

Illustrated by Anahit Aleksanyan

Copyright/Legal Page information:
Moments with Massy series
Moving Away Will Be Okay!
Carte-Sears, Kellie
Moving Away Will Be Okay!/written by Kellie Carte-Sears ; illustrated by Anahit Aleksanyan
Publisher Sears Enterprises LLC

Summary: Although wise and compassionate for her young age, when Massy learns
she is moving she finds herself consumed by emotions and filled with questions.
But her loveable cat Blue, guides her through the process in a mindful, lighthearted,
and playful way. Together, their journey leads them to understanding and happiness.

Interest age level: 04-10.

Issued also as an ebook.

ISBN: 978-1-7923-2742-1 (binding hardcover)
ISBN: 978-1-7923-8 (eBK)

1.Change-Juvenile fiction. Moving, 2.Household Juvenile fiction.
3.Adjustment (Psychology) in children-Juvenile fiction. 4.Moving, Household-Fiction.
5.Change-Fiction. 6.Adjustment (Psychology)-Fiction

First published by:
Sears Enterprises LLC 10 Bethany Dr.   Fremont, Ohio 43420

Printed in the United States of America.

Are you feeling worried?
Do you wonder where you'll stay?
Are you packing up your stuff?
Are you **moving far away?**

Are your parents in a tizzy?
Does it make you wonder why?
Well, moving can be difficult;
it's hard to say goodbye.

Let's talk about how moving
makes you feel deep down inside.
It's good to **share your feelings**;
there's no reason you should hide.

I know it isn't easy when you must
leave your home behind,
and you're not sure of where you're going
or what you just might find.

When you tell your friends
you're moving,
they won't like the news at all,
but give them all your number,
and tell them
they can call!

It's okay that you have questions;
asking questions isn't wrong!
And talking to your parents
helps you as you move along.

You'll miss your home;
you'll miss your friends-
so many things to miss-
it's hard to understand it all —
a big change such as this.

Making changes can be scary,
but perhaps you didn't know,
that everyone must go through change,
for change is how we **grow.**

Some things that change
will happen fast,
but some of them will not –
let's make a game of
naming them;
we'll **both** give this a shot!

Your house will **change**,
your room will **change**,
you'll even **change** your street;
you can decorate and **change** the style
to make it super neat!

There's one thing that will not change —
think hard! I know you'll guess.
Your friends and family love you,
no matter your address!

I see you're really good at this fun game
that we've been playing –
let's guess which things are **going**
and which things will be **staying**.

Your favorite toys and all your clothes
are things you'll want to pack,
but leave the kitchen sink behind –
it won't fit inside the sack!

And no matter what you do,
don't leave **the books
you love to read**,
but that big oak tree in the yard?
That's staying, we've agreed.

Let's take the little rocking horse,
since that's **your favorite seat,**
but leave that rusty mailbox
in the front yard
by the street.

Though you'll have to leave your neighbors,
you won't have to feel alone;
you can always call them up,
for you're sure to **take your phone!**

Be sure to take along with you
the things you really like–
your **fishing pole**,
your roller skates,
your shiny **purple bike**.

Bring with you my scratching post
and favorite jingle ball–
when we get to **our new home,**
I'll bat it down the hall.

Check the shelves inside your closet,
and look beneath your bed.
You'll be surprised at what you find –
oh look!
I found your sled!

Clean the things and
sort them out,
then put them in a box;
keep them neat and tidy –
you should even
fold your socks!

SOCKS

T-SHIRTS

Then load them in the moving truck;
it's time to make your move!
Do you feel excited yet?
Are you getting in the groove?

Moving is a change, for sure,
but it comes with a reward –
it's like playing a guitar
when you strum a brand new chord.

Do you feel thrilled to think about
a new place to explore?

As you look for **the surprises**
behind every
brand new door?

Moving is a new adventure,
so don't let your heart be sad;
think of all the friends you'll meet,
and that will make your **heart feel glad.**

"Home is where the heart is" –
I've often heard it said before.
It's the place where you're surrounded
by the people you adore.

Get that warm and fuzzy feeling,
knowing you are safe and sound,
As you make yourself feel right at home,
the place **where love is found.**

A house is just a building –
people build them everywhere,
but a home is filled with
love and warmth
for everyone to share.

So even though you're moving
and although it may be far,
you've left a house
but not your home,

for **home** is
where **you**
are.

REVIEWS AND RECOMMENDATIONS

"What a creative way to put a child's worry at ease! The story explores helpful ways to remedy what could be a very anxious time in a child's life. Children and parents will enjoy reading as Massy resolves her worries about moving. I look forward to more Moments with Massy."

Melanie Allen
Director - Sandusky County Department of Job and Family Services

"I really enjoyed reading it (Moving Away Will Be Okay!) and feel that the content will be helpful for children struggling with transitioning to a new home. Rhyming provides a nice beat that often times stimulates a child's attention and keeps them interested as well as enhances their ability to recall information and content. I also found it important that the uneasy feelings of the child experiencing the move were validated in the book. This helps normalize the difficulty that moving presents to many children and adults. I also enjoyed how the story progressed to recognizing that there would in fact, be changes but recognized that change does not have to result in all things negative. I found that the end of the story presented a sense of hope for a child that their new house can transition into a new home."

Patti Schwan MSW, LISW-S
Counseling and Therapy - ProMedica Physicians Behavioral Health

"Children open their understanding when they find that others face challenges similar to theirs. Kellie Carte-Sears has created a story that will help children meet the challenges of insecurity during a home moving process. What a delightful story!"

Joyce Hall-Yates, J.D.
Vice Provost, Dean, School of Arts & Sciences
Tiffin University

"Kellie Carte-Sears' new book Moving Away Will Be Okay! has what so many well-intended and often beautiful children's books often miss—a protagonist (Massy) who is wise and compassionate for her young age, but an example for young readers and listeners as they journey through what can be a fairly traumatic experience for children—moving! With all the adventure, visual beauty, and rhythm of a great kid's book, Moving Away Will Be Okay! also gently guides a child through what might at first seem scary to a point where they come to see the experience as an adventure, and the place they arrive as --home--.
A must for any family on the move!"

Rodney Miles Taber, Author

"I felt that it (Moving Away Will Be Okay!) was very engaging to young children and will do well at keeping the children entertained and interested in the story. I think that this will be an excellent resource for children."

Dr. Stephanie Tiell DNP, APRN, FNP-C, PMHNP-BC
Child Psychiatry – ProMedica Physicians Behavioral Health

ABOUT AUTHOR

YEARS AGO, when KELLIE CARTE-SEARS learned her young grandchildren were moving
to a different city from where she lived, she decided the best way to assist them
with this change was to find a book that would help them embrace their emotions and
let them know everything would be okay - a book that would show them moving didn't
have to be so scary but could be fun and adventurous. But she couldn't find a book that
was "real" in a way that her grandchildren would personally connect.
So Kellie went home and wrote her first book Moving Away Will Be Okay!
Shortly after, she wrote her second book, You're Not Bad, We All Get Mad!
and has other books already underway.

Kellie Carte-Sears has been an entrepreneur for over 30 years starting businesses
as a way to solve problems. Her drive to fulfill market gaps and the needs of others
has gained her great success on many different platforms. Her newest book series,
Moments with Massy ™ is no different. She has a Bachelor's degree in Business
Administration from Tiffin University and Associate of Arts degrees in both Social and
Behavioral Science as well as Psychology from Terra State Community College.

Kellie's insights, experiences, and psychological comprehension as it relates to positive
interaction and behavior, provides her with an ability to directly understand and connect
with others. Using the talents and gifts God has given her, she is offering her books
as a way to assist children during life changes and challenges.

Moments
with
massy

™